RACHEL'S CRY

A Journey Through Grief

by

Richard A. Dew, M.D.

TENNESSEE VALLEY
Publishing

Knoxville, Tennessee
1996

Published by Tennessee Valley Publishing,
P. O. Box 52527, Knoxville, TN 37950

Printed and bound in the United States of America.
Second Printing

Library of Congress Catalog Card Number: 96-60727

ISBN 1-882194-19-5

Copies of this book may be purchased for $10 plus $2 shipping and handling. Please order from:

> Tennessee Valley Publishing
> P.O. Box 52527-2527
> Knoxville, TN 37950
>
> E-mail: tvp1@ix.netcom.com
> Telephone 423-584-5235
> Facsimile 423-584-0113

To Jean and Greg,
who have proven far stronger than I,
and to Brad.

Special thanks to Don, Suzie, Tom, Margaret and my other compassionate friends who walked with me, to Ken, Ann, Larry and Carolyn who held my hand, to Joel and David who listened to me, and to Ron, Geron, Sandra and Ruth Cates who encouraged me to write.

A cry is heard in Ramah,
Lamentation and bitter weeping,
Rachel, weeping for her children,
Refusing to be comforted,
Because they are no more.

Jerimiah 31:15

CONTENTS

Dear Reader,

My son, Bradley Morris Dew, was a student at Millsaps College in Jackson, Mississippi. While returning from work on June 7, 1992, he was randomly selected by two young thugs, chased down and brutally murdered. He was 21 years old.

These poems were written in response to this event and its effect on me, my family and my world. They spring from my personal experiences as I went through grief, sometimes alone, sometimes with my family and often in the company of fellow mourners in The Compassionate Friends. That I am not a professional poet is obvious. My goal in writing these poems was primarily self-therapy. However, I hope sharing them might help others who are struggling through grief. Finally, I hope that the public at large might come to better understand those who grieve.

Sincerely,

Richard A. Dew, M.D.

An Ordinary Day

It was just another day.
No one special came.
Nothing unusual happened.
The evening was the same.
Just an ordinary day
And then the telephone rang.
From that moment on forever
Everything was changed.

Grave Words

I lie awake
In the wake
Of the wake,
Trying to hold
The whole
Of the hole.

Travelers

Grief is a long
And lonely trip
On which everyone
Carries his own
Personal baggage.

Going Through Grief

Grief moves in orderly stages we're told.
In stepwise fashion we slowly progress
Through Shock, Denial, Disorganized Stress,
One after another we feel them unfold.
Next we are Angry for all that is gone,
Then we become Guilty, Depressed and Bereaved.
After which we Recover, our friends are relieved,
Our grief is over and we can move on.
But it really isn't like that at all.
Grief moves erratically in fits and starts,
In multiple stages sometimes we stall,
Dragging and creeping at a deadening crawl.
In time dawns the knowledge that chills our hearts,
Grief may get lighter, but it never departs.

Shock Treatment

It all began like a kick in the gut.
Then like ripples from a pebble spread
A nauseating numbness, all senses shut
Down, stunned, inert, frozen and dead.
Out of body existing, floating, removed,
Hovering and looking downward at me,
As I received friends and those whom I loved
And sat in a daze hearing your eulogy.
Distracted, unhearing, barely aware
Of the world that's around me, I get up each day
And plod through from morning till bedtime where
I drop to my knees and desperately pray,
    "Please let me stay in this unfeeling void
    And not have to face my life that's destroyed."

Denial

It's just a bad dream, a nightmare more near.
You can't convince me he'll never come back.
I rode with him there and helped him unpack
When he went to school earlier this year.
Any day he will be driving back home,
Tall tales to tell with a twinkling eye.
No, he hasn't called, he hasn't said why
It's been so long, but I know that he'll come.
Remove all his pictures, don't say his name,
Reminders just make the tears start to flow.
I'll just keep pretending and trying to do
All that I can to keep things the same
And not to admit it. For, what I know
In my head, my heart can't handle as true.

Confounded, Confused
and All Stressed Out

Life whirls around me, nothing stands still.
A dozen dilemmas diverge in my brain.
I can find nothing to hold onto until
I'm sane, the only thing constant is pain.
Restless, in motion, moving about,
With wrenching reminders I pause to weep,
Keyed up and listless, hyped and worn out,
Fatigued to the bone but unable to sleep.
Why? Why? Why? Nobody can tell me why.
If God, my faith and my prayers can't lift
Me up, is all that I lived by a lie?
My anchors have broken. I am adrift,
    Forgetful and frazzled, control all gone,
    Searching and asking, helpless, alone.

Anger Most Foul

A tiny larva, it started to grow,
Gnawing and boring deep in my soul,
Creating a rot at my core, anger so
Subtly spreading, taking control,
Then lashing out wildly at anyone who
Crossed my path. Neighbor or stranger all the same,
With no logic or reason outward it flew,
Randomly seeking someone to blame.
Finally it focused much more nearby,
At God and my friends and my family
And at him who allowed himself to die.
Then lastly I heaped my rage upon me.
    Now from my mirror glare the angry eyes
    Of a stranger I don't even recognize.

Guilty as Sin

A father's supposed to shield and protect
His children from harm. Because of this I've
Tortured myself facing up to the fact
That my child is dead and I'm still alive.
Was it punishment for some long past sin?
Why didn't I warn him? I should have known.
I might have prevented it if I had been
There. At least he wouldn't have died alone.
At rare times when I laugh, I'm full of shame
For having fun. I can easily see
That logically I am not to blame,
But I can't convince my psyche and me.
    In times of reflection I wonder why
    If God can forgive me, then why can't I?

Down and Depressed

Through tear-filled pools into darkness staring
Back at times now dead and gone. What's ahead
To me seems bleak, I am long past caring,
In these dreary hours from which sleep has fled.
Daylight's no better, it seems that my eyes
Selectively filter and screen the light,
Making gloomy the world and gray the skies,
Matching my mood. There's no hope in sight.
I can barely get up, work is a chore,
Profound fatigue permeates all of me.
Still I plod on, I'm not sure what for,
There's no point or meaning that I can see.
    Each monotonous day it seems that I
    Am just marking time until I die.

Turning Point

Dawn does not so much break as it happens.
Dark slides into light so slowly my eyes
Adjust without thought, as faint pink ribbons
Turn to streamers of orange in eastern skies.
So goes my grief with no strident fanfare.
Sadness and grieving have been all I know,
Then, for a brief moment, it is not there.
Imperceptibly then the moments grow,
Until I laugh without guilt. Life's more worthwhile,
I don't feel as compelled to visit the grave.
I can remember some good times and I smile.
There was nothing dramatic and I have
    Had no revelation, no special thing.
    I just felt a bit better sometime last spring.

Restoration

Emerging from the maelstrom of grief, you
Pause and take stock. Like tempered, Toledo steel
Made stronger by passing through fire, I feel
Quietly confident, transformed and new.
Life is more vital, death no more holds fear,
A gentle calm pervades much that I do.
I'm wiser, knowing what others can't know,
Priorities are straight, perspectives clear.
My wounds have healed, I am ready to go
Back into life, seeking people once more.
Glad that I'm "normal" again, all of them
Welcome me back, not knowing that, although
I may almost seem like I was before,
My soul has deep scars and walks with a limp.

Cliché Comfort

I can imagine
From a past ordeal.
I've been there before.
I know just how you feel.
   I am sure that you
   Think that you do
   .....But you don't.

It must be God's will.
His time had just come.
He's living with God.
God called him back home.
   If your theology
   Is to uplift me.
   .....It doesn't.

And this too shall pass.
Soon it will be gone.
Time heals all wounds.
But life must go on.
   I know you believe
   That time will relieve,
   .....But it won't.

Get hold of yourself.
Don't dwell on the past.
Count all your blessings.
Don't be so downcast.
   I know that I should,
   I would if I could,
   .....But I can't.

Personal Effects

Still stunned, I stare, and a shudder
Ripples slowly down my spine.
Pigeons perch and wheel and flutter
Around the bird-shit splattered sign
Carved in stone: Jackson City Jail.
Dazed, I go through the oaken door
Into a hall once painted pale
Blue, anxious to complete my chore.
With other bits of human debris,
I'm washed sluggishly along
To a desk in a back eddy
Only to find I have come the wrong
Way. So with flowing city flotsam
I'm swept back the way I came,
Aimlessly drifting, my brain numb,
Then all at once, a desk marked "Claims."
"What's your name?" grunts the man in blue.
"Oh...you..I'm sorry," he blurts out.
Fumbling, he files a form or two.
"Get out here, Joe," he gives a shout,
"This stuff is ready for release."
Joe departs and comes briskly back
And calmly hands me a large piece
Of my life in a brown paper sack.

Two Weeks After

The sun rose in the east today,
The morning paper was on time,
The car pool next door honked away,
The neighbor's wash was on the line.
Rush hour traffic whizzed on by
As I drove into work alone,
Watching others blithely try
To drive and prattle on the phone.
Those at work dash to and fro,
About their mundane tasks they go.
Don't they know? Don't they care? He's dead!
How can the world bustle ahead
With business as usual?
Damn them! Damn them! Damn them all!

Night Cry

The sky's pitch black, the stars are hid,
Clouds cover the moon like a shroud.
Stumbling, she staggers on amid
Winter bare trees, weeping aloud.
Memories like demons tear at her mind,
They pierce her heart like a knife.
There is no peace or comfort to find
In this the midnight of her life.
Within her seething brain he's near,
Yet sobbing shouts get no reply.
Only the dark is there to hear
Her haunting, wailing, keening cry,
    Echoing some prehistoric rite,
    As she calls his name in the night.

Tough Questions

"What shall we do with the body?" they said.
"Will you accompany him or ship him ahead?
What funeral home should we notify?
Do you wish him dressed in a coat and tie?
Would you prefer wood or metal coffin?
What kind of a crypt should we put it in?

What would you like in the obituary?
In what newspaper do you want it to be?
When did he die and when was he born?
Who are the kinfolk who'll be there to mourn?
Have any pictures? What did he do?
Who will the gifts and donations go to?

Will services be at both church and grave?
Do you want the flower tags to save?
Will all of the family in pews combine?
Will you receive friends? Who'll stand in the line?
What type of tunes should the organist play?
What songs will be sung and what shall I say?

Where on the hill do you want him to lie?
A place in full view for those who pass by?
Should the marker be flat or stand upright?
What's the inscription you want us to write?
Do you want to purchase perpetual care?
Would you like flowers daily to be placed there?

Would you let the insurer investigate?
With this offer could we negotiate?
You know of course that's a last resort?
Won't you get them an autopsy report?
Don't you know what's required in this state?
Could you get us a Death Certificate?

How is your wife doing and how are you?
Do you have anything that I can do?
After six months aren't you over it yet?
Isn't it time that you turn loose and get
Back into life and move on from here?
Are you going to grieve for another year?

Do you have children? How many are there?
Do they all live here and, if not, then where?
Oh, how did he die? What happened to him?
My grandkids pictures...like to see them?
Aren't you lucky to have other children now?
Would you in remembrance his school endow?"

Will I remember and never forget?
Will troubling dreams my sleep always upset?
Can I ever remember and not feel pain?
Where is he now? Will I see him again?
Will I think of him and smile and not cry?
Don't I know that even young people die?

Why?

Jumbled Journey

Oh, God, no! Not that. Don't let it be.
It's not true! I'm dreaming. Not my child. Not he.

I'm calm at the funeral. I don't even cry.
I'm holding up well. I'm sure I'll get by.

Dazed and confused, I'm coming apart.
Struggling to function. Where do I start?

Damn! Damn! Damn! Damn all the world and you!
You seem to know all of the wrong things to say and do!

Why? Why? Why? Won't somebody please tell me why?
What a stupid answer! Go away! I want to die.

I must have. I should have. I caused him to go.
If only. Why didn't I? It's my fault I know.

I can't! I won't! I'm too tired. I'll weep.
Leave me alone. I just want to sleep.

I sit and do nothing. I bitch and I moan.
I'm sad and depressed. I'm better alone.

My marriage has changed. I'm no help to her.
We grieve mainly alone, not together.

I'm just a bit better. At times I will smile.
I move forward an inch. I slip backward a mile.

Two years he's been gone. I'm still alive.
I resolve to go on. I will survive.
I'm deeper and stronger than I used to be.
My journey through heartbreak has forged a new me.
But a shadow of grief will tinge life sad
Until I rejoin the part of me, that went with Brad.

Memories

Two decades of life shared together,
"I couldn't forget!" just a trite cliché,
As I struggle and strain to remember
Bits and snatches of one single day.

I intended to keep me a journal,
But in busyness my intentions ignored.
Now my brain frantically reaches and searches
For data I lost and did not record.

If I had just jotted a daily reminder,
A word, a brief note, a vignette,
And not blithely believed it impossible
That in anyway I could forget.

Yet elusive as a swallowtail,
A past moment flutters around.
A will-o-the-wisp, a wafting mist,
Sensed, glimpsed, felt, but not quite found.

I can recite a poem my father read me.
I still hum a song I long ago heard.
But I cannot with all my power recall
When he started to talk, or what was his first word.

He was supposed to keep memories for me,
And by him they would be told.
Too late I learned I expected
Remembering by youth for the old.

How Do You Say Good-by

If a fir when it falls in the forest
Makes no noise if no one is near,
How do you say good-by
When no one is there to hear?

Who do you say good-by to
When the person who's leaving is gone,
And all that is left are the memories
That you live and re-live all alone?
You say good-by to the little guy
You taught how to ride a bike,
And good-by to the heart-bonded buddy
Who went with you to hunt, fish and hike.
And finally good-by to your hero
Who would be all that you wanted to be,
Who'd climb to heights never dreamed of
And see sights that you'd never see.

Where do you say good-by
When you don't know where he is?
Where can you go and feel him close by
And not lost in some dark abyss?
You can say good-by in his bedroom
Where you snuggled and read stories to him,
Or down by the creek in the deep woods
Where you taught him to fish and to swim.
You can say good-by by the goal posts
Where he made you feel so proud,
Or out on the lake in a bass boat
Where you debated the shape of a cloud.

What do you say good-by to
When nothing is there to see?
Do you just talk to the air, or murmur a prayer
That something's there listening that's he?
You say good-by to your future
That you had planned and barely begun,
And to the joy and happiness of grandkids
When you finally admit there'll be none.
And you say good-by to the good times
And birthdays and Christmas cheer,
And, hopefully, good-by to That Day
Which methodically comes round each year.

How do you say good-by
And accept that it's over and done?
When you can deny it no more, you must close the door
And whisper, "Good-by until then, my son."

They've Got Each Other

Quiet comes the dawn through curtained windows,
Quiet as their breathing, pretending sleep.
Carefully not touching, for fear stray
Spasms betray silent sadness and sobbing,
Or, even worse, be misconstrued as a
Prelude to intimacy and rejected.
Finally, stirring with elaborate
Stretching and yawning, they confront the day.
"How did you sleep?" "Fine, and you?" "Okay."
Quickly completing the morning ritual,
Newly self-conscious they dress. At breakfast
They speak in simple questions and answers,
Avoiding sharing, lest control be lost.
With an automatic, chaste peck on the cheek
They part with a secret sigh of relief.

"How could you possibly
Think about that?
And with him barely
Six months gone from us?
You men are all alike.
You have no conception.
Don't you understand?
Nine long months in me,
I carried him there.
I nursed and nurtured,
Now nothing. I'm numb.
I can't just pick up
And get back into
Life and work and sex.

"Damn! Why'd I do that?
I knew she wasn't
In the mood for romance.
She never is anymore.
It's not enough
That I've lost a son,
I've lost my wife, too.
Doesn't she realize?
My future is gone.
I am so lonesome.
I need to hold her
And be held in return.
Am I now so repulsive
We can't even touch?

Why don't you talk
To me? You're like a lump.
Sullen and surly
You snap off my head
If I mention his name.
You don't even cry.
You haven't been back
To the grave. Not once!
I don't think you care.
You sit and mope or
You just work, work, work.
What's the matter with you?"

Why won't she stop talking?
It tears me apart
To constantly dwell on him.
It's all I can do
To not break down and cry.
Must she visit the grave?
I can't stand that place!
I need to be alone.
With some peace and quiet
I can make it through.
Thank God, I have my work.
What's the matter with her?"

"How was your day?" "Fine, and yours?" "Okay."
Stiffly the afternoon ritual is done.
After another question and answer meal
And an awkward, near wordless evening
Of vacantly reading and watching TV,
With reluctance they rise and retire to rest.
"Help me," she silently screams at him.
"Hold and console me," his soundless reply.
Suppressing the love they're desperate to keep,
They motionless lie and mutely weep.
Quiet comes the night through curtained windows,
Quiet as their breathing pretending sleep.

Come Away

Come, my child, and go with me,
We'll do all the things that we planned.
Things will be like they used to be,
We'll run and we'll play hand-in-hand.
Hurry, my child, I'll go with you
To places that we've never been,
Many new things we'll see and do,
We'll laugh and be happy again.
Oh, no, my child, don't stay behind,
And leave me to live all alone.
I think that I'll go out of my mind
With nothing to touch but a stone.

Separation

From where I stand
I cannot see
How far it is
From you to me.
At different times
It seems to be
A step   or an infinity.

Dog Days

The dog days of grief are here,
Sapping all strength and energy,
Empty of any joy or cheer,
The longest most painful time of the year,
 Dragging, dragging endlessly.

Too tired to work, too tired to move,
Spent from fruitless attempts to cope,
With loss of presence, loss of love,
Loss of guidance from above,
 Seeking, seeking a ray of hope.

Mind and body are filled with pain,
Mental unrest beyond belief,
In constant struggle, constant strain
To keep on living, to stay sane,
 Praying, praying for relief.

Throughout the night to lie and weep,
From the subconscious there are drawn
Emotions that are dark and deep,
And memories well up, preventing sleep,
 Waiting, waiting for the dawn.

To Know or Not

I wept I never had the chance
In which to say good-bye.
But would it have sat more lightly
Had I known you were to die?

I've often pondered late at night
About which would hurt the most,
Anticipation of your leaving,
Or acceptance of your loss.

Painful Pleasure

It hurts so much to remember,
But to relive those moments again
Is the closest I come to pleasure,
Yet it's not very different from pain.

Then why hold so hard to memories
That are painful and make me upset?
If I let myself stop hurting,
I'm afraid that I will forget.

Multiple Losses

Much more than he died when he died.
With him died: Hopes and dreams of future things,
Vacations and visits and homecomings,
Grandchildren who would be my pride,
Security when I lay down at night,
The assurance of another day,
Some time to say what I meant to say,
A tomorrow in which to make things right,
Attempting the things we had hoped to try,
Finishing projects we planned to do,
One last "I'm sorry" or "I love you,"
Another chance to hug and say good-by.
I find when I look behind the shroud,
Death comes not alone but in a crowd.

Looking Back

It happened so quickly I couldn't think,
One minute you're here, the next one you're gone.
Today, here laughing, then lost in a blink.
Your life was over before it'd begun.
My thoughts are all jumbled, I'm on the brink
Of insanity. Where are you, My son?
    I can't concentrate, the world's all a blur.
    I just want things to go back like they were.

Life is disrupted, I'm drowning in grief,
Falling into a pit of despair.
I kneel and I call on all past belief,
To the heavens I shout a desperate prayer.
I hide in my work, my home time is brief,
My family needs me and I am not there.
    I love my wife but I'm useless to her.
    Dear God, let things go back like they were.

I've struggled through grief, fiercely fought pain,
I've wrestled and sought to understand why.
Why is there evil? Why are innocents slain?
Why is there sickness? And why do kids die?
I whispered and roared these questions in vain.
A deathly cold silence, was my reply.
    From this I believe I can safely infer,
    That things will never go back like they were.

Through all this turmoil, I've deepened and grown,
I am more caring than I was back then,
I have learned things I would never have known,
I am someone I would never have been.
My new faith is more solid than that which has flown,
I think I now have a new place to begin.
    While it may not be the way I prefer
    I'll survive and go on, though things aren't like they were.

Dream Death

There's a secret place in the back of my heart,
I found it when we said good-bye.
A portion of this I've set apart,
A place where my dreams go to die.

My dreams for your future, the joy that we'd share,
My pride as you grew and went out on your own,
The wife you would have, the children you'd rear,
My legacy you'd carry when I had gone.

Some dreams go easily, some of them not.
Some angrily stomp in, some quietly slip by.
But eventually they all discover the spot
In the back of my heart ......where they die.

The Psychiatrist

"How are things going since we last met?"

"Everything is the same. Nothing's changed yet."

His eyes visibly glaze as once again
I tear out my heart, hold it in my hand,
And to my secret Shaman I bare my soul,
Retelling again what I've already told.

"You realize, of course, this has lasted too long.
You must pull yourself up, let go and move on.
He's been dead six months and you still cry.
Write a letter to him. Tell him good-by."

Uncomfortable pause, then another try,

"Have you taken your medicine as prescribed?"

I watch as his lips soundlessly form words,
Trying to concentrate and pretend I heard
What he said.
                    "Yes, my Valium, Prozac,
And Elavil, too. The pain's just as bad,
But now I can't tell where it is that I hurt.
I sleep a bit longer, but the dreams are the same."

"What is it you want?" he says with a sigh.

"I want my son back. I want to know why
He died. Since that is not possible,
I want someone to listen and understand,
Who'll cry along with me and hold my hand,
And will let me be as sad as I choose
Without giving advice. Who won't leave when I lose
My temper. Who'll hear without judging when
I rail at God and ask where has He been.
I want you to care, then, if you see fit,
Break my heart gently. Don't smash it to bits."

Exhausted, I slump back down in my seat,
Spent and empty, my tirade complete.

Unmoved, with owl-eyes he stares at me,
Looks at his watch then casually
Says,
        "We should increase your dosage a pill or two."

Ambivalence

He plods along dancing, his happy heart sad.
Painful, fond memories his raised spirits weigh down.
Joy and grief fill his mind, living a past that is dead.

Raised to the night sky, smiling face streaked with tears,
Cursing, he fervently offers his prayers
To the cruel loving God he seeks and avoids.

His feet firmly rooted in soft, shifting sand,
With fear-laden confidence the future he'll meet,
Shakily secure knowing life's bittersweet.

Memories

Memories have two sides:
What was, what was to be.
I don't know which hurts most
Of this duality.

Looking Back

When the
Future seems gone
We look to the past, preferring sweet dreams of then
To the nightmare
Of now.

Mary Cried

Mary cried on Christmas,
To her just his birthing day,
Sifting through her memories
Of silly pranks and things he'd say.

She lived her life as best she could
With dreams of all that might have been.
At times she'd even laugh and sing,
The pain would start to ease and then

Passover came and her heart would break
On that Friday that was not Good,
That awful day that always left her
Depressed and down and black in mood.

Though Easter made life bearable,
Until she grew old and died,
As she reminisced on
Christmas day, Mary cried.

Too Soon

There's much more about you that I'd like to know.
Let's sit and talk to the end of the day.
Please don't leave me, it's too soon to go.

What were you thinking when gazing out so
Pensive and thoughtful, your mind far away?
There's much more about you that I'd like to know.

Hunting and fishing, a romp in the snow,
Basketball, baseball and football we'll play.
Please don't leave me, it's too soon to go.

Did I love you enough? Did I help your mind grow?
Did I set an example that helped show you the way?
There's much more about you that I'd like to know.

I understand about life's ebb and flow,
But you've just begun yours. You must stay.
Please don't leave me, it's too soon to go.

The fact that you're gone my head knows, although
My heart makes me nightly kneel down and pray,
"There's much more about you that I'd like to know.
Please don't leave me, it's too soon to go."

Christmas Eve

Silent night, holy night...

"It's about time, "he says quietly.
Deliberately, wordlessly,
They gather the materials
Carefully put away last year,
The matches, candle, candle jar
To fend off the harsh winter wind.

Tis the season to be jolly...

Slowly they drive toward the town's edge,
Past homes with bright, blinking bulbs.
Cars of faraway relatives
Fill their drives. Happy, laughing
Families, children home from school,
Pass by on the way to midnight Mass.

It's the most wonderful time of the year...

At last, town lights left far behind,
They sit mute, each wrapped in private
Cocoons of memories of Christmas past,
Excited whispers from their room,
Silly giggles, fervent good-night
Kisses, anticipation of morning.

On a cold winter's night that was so deep...

Through the gate, down the drive, engine killed.
Frozen grass crunching underfoot
Hand-in-hand they walk up the hill
To the familiar moonlit stone.
With practiced hands they brush it clean,
Then prepare their votive Noel.

The world in solemn stillness lay...

Lump in throat, arm-in- arm,
Candle lit, they stand and weep,
But not so bitter as in years past.
The pain's as deep but not so long,
As once again they dream of things
That should have been but never were.

The stars in the sky look down where he lay...

"Let's go," he says. She nods assent.
They leave, though turn back once to see
The lonely flame of their lost boy
Gleaming peacefully through the dark.
He whispers softly, his visit done,
"Merry Christmas and good-night, my son."

Sleep in heavenly peace,
Sleep in heavenly peace.

Wardrobes

Blue blazer, gray slacks,
Dark socks with black shoes,
White shirt, red tie,
They're easy to choose.

But it's hard to decide
What my demeanor will be
For those whom I meet
And who speak to me.

Smiling or laughing?
Maybe both combined?
Optimistic, positive,
To show that I'm fine?

I can't let my face
Give true feelings away.
So which of my masks
Shall I wear today?

Getting Even

In secret hours from midnight to dawn,
Daytime scruples left behind,
And thoughts of sleep now long since gone,
I see what demons I can find
In nooks and crannies of my mind.

All virtues sealed up tight and hid,
Relishing thoughts of how to try
To even scores for what they did,
Tooth for tooth and eye for eye,
By sword to live and sword to die.

Through vapors murderous I seek
Vengeance pits and hatred holes.
Down slimy corridors that reek
Of tortured souls on beds of coals,
Revenge my brain alone controls.

Visions of those I would destroy
On my eyelids I clearly see.
For a heart now bereft of joy
Payment I want, personally.
Merciful God, have pity on me.

Dead Dreams

What can you do with a dream that is dead?
Try to forget? Kick it under the bed?
Push it deep down, out of sight out of mind?
Keep it hid back in a place you can't find?
Cling to it frantically, don't let it go?
Pretend it's still there, even if you know
That what you have left is the mummified husk
Of a dead dream that comes and haunts you at dusk?

You cannot bury your dreams when they die,
Or leave them around haphazard to lie.
You gather and save with the tenderest of care
Each shattered shard of the dream that was there.
With a mixture of tears and hope and pain
You fit what you can back together again
And see what peace it can impart
From a treasured place on the shelf of your heart.

Awkward Silence

I wish that someone would say his name.
I know my feelings they're trying to spare,
And so we go through the charade, the game,

Of dancing around the ghost that is there,
Trying to avoid evoking a tear,
Or stirring emotions too painful to bear.

That he be forgotten is what I fear,
That no one will even his presence miss,
As if there were no trace that he was here.

By referring to him, my purpose is
Not to stir pity or keep things the same.
But my heart will simply break if his

Memory will die like a flickering flame.
I just wish someone would say his name.

One Moment in Time

If you could pick
One moment in time
To have and live over again,
Could you decide
Which one to choose
Out of all the days that have been?

Would it be a time
When they were cuddly and young
And totally dependent on you?
Or when they progressed
And went out on their own
And spread their wings and they flew?

Or when rebellion was theirs
And you wanted to help
But held back, not to overprotect?
Would you leave out the hurts
That when healed helped us grow
And deepened our love and respect?

I could not select
One moment in time.
I wouldn't know which one to choose.
I'll just live in the faith
That in some time to come
All of our moments will fuse

Into a joyful reunion
When time is no more,
No present, no future, no past,
And all of the dreams
That were taken away
Will be shared together at last.

His Room

Sun splinters through
The stained-glass unicorn
Still on the sill,
Splattering blank walls with color.
Few things are as forlorn
As a vacant room,
Furniture gone,
Awaiting definition.
Bare, yet there on the carpet
Imprints of chair and waterbed,
And there is the hole he
Accidentally shot through the wall,
And there, and there, and there,
Nail holes that held
Pictures and posters
And eight-pointed antlers,
And there.........God, how can a place
So empty be so full?

The Bone Yard

The echoing drums of the Masai
Tell a story fantastic to hear.
How aging and injured elephants
Slip away when their dying is near

To a place that's deep in the jungle,
Known only to natives in legend.
Quietly or bellowing defiance,
They enter and there their lives end.

Dreams are similar to elephants.
They are noble, long-lived and strong,
But when they are mortally wounded,
They go to the place they belong.

Inevitably drawn there by instinct,
In secret they lie down and die,
And there in the midst of their dream kin
Their bleached bones are mingled to lie.

The souls of the dreamers are empty,
They wander in search of their dreams,
For something that gives their lives meaning
And their sense of purpose redeems.

Some give up and quit, some hide in work,
Some turn to drink, some kneel in prayer,
While others doggedly persist in
Hunting the dreams they hope are still there.

Sometimes they find the lost bone yard.
They sift through the rubble and then
From the remnants of dreams that they
Find there, they rebuild their lives again.

The Sampler

Carefully stitched and knitted
By our controlling hand,
A design just to our liking,
A pattern we had planned.
Comfortable, familiar,
Held up for all to see,
A source of pride and pleasure
Defining who are we.
Thus double our consternation,
When tragedy arrives
And relentlessly unravels
The fabric of our lives.

Parents

Problems, dilemmas,
Flat tires, dead lights,
Father, the fixer,
Making things right.

Scraped knees, hurt feelings,
A painful ordeal,
Nurturing mother,
Helping things heal.

When Death comes calling,
What will they do
To cope with disaster
And get themselves through

The Hell of their lives
Going up in smoke,
And the healer is sick
And the fixer is broke?

Ecclesiasticus

In life there is an ebb and flow,
A time to come, a time to go.
A need to turn loose and hold on
To memories of times long since gone.
An urge to leave the past, and yet
A fear of moving lest we forget.
An interchange of joy and tears,
Acceptance of both cribs and biers.
A sense of triumph and defeat
In knowing life is both bitter and sweet.

Fairy Tale

For many years I dwelt secure
In the belief that good begets good,
That if you did the things you should,
Life would be rich, success was sure.
A kind, benevolent God would bless
And protect your loved ones from any
Harm. He'd provide you with many
Days of pleasure and happiness.
My world went on smoothly because
I clung to this simple credo.
There was seldom a reason for more
Than a fleeting doubt. But that was
Once upon a time - long, long ago -
In a life that I lived before.

The Beyond

Nestled in her loving arms,
Newborn baby, warm and wet,
Quick, tell me where did you come from
Before you grow and you forget.

Cradled in her clinging arms,
Fading child who cannot stay,
Please, tell me where you are bound for
Before you've died and gone away.

They come to us from somewhere,
And for a while remain,
Then they return to somewhere else,
Or are the two the same?

Continuity

Before we were born, we were,
Then for a brief time, we are,
After we are not, yet we are,
And beyond that, we will be,
But never shall we "have been."

Stillborn

With love I conceived and I bore you,
I dreamt of you when I was a child.
As I felt you grow I adored you,
With your first feeble flutter I smiled.

Happily I hummed an old lullaby,
While I readied your room and layette.
With thumps and bumps I felt you reply,
Playing percussion in a happy duet.

Each day that passed our future I planned,
Where we would go and things we would do.
We'd take trips to the beach and play in the sand
And go to the circus and visit the zoo!

Nine joyful months together we spent,
Looking ahead to all that would be.
Quickly you came, and just as quick went,
And the two of us now is just me.

A past that has passed, a future that's gone,
Everyone's back to normal again.
While here I am, lost and alone,
Torn by thoughts of what might have been.

Memories die out like an ember,
I struggle to hold them, and yet,
It's very hard to remember,
When you were not here to forget.

*Dedicated to those whose legitimate losses are discounted
or ignored. Who have few, if any, memories to offset their
shattered hopes and dreams.*

Night Noises

Uneasiness comes with the night,
With the sounds we hear in the dark:

The soft exchange of baby breath,
Which compulsively, anxiously,
We bend down to hear or to feel,

A cry or a cough with illness,
Made much more menacing by our
Runaway imaginations,

Frightened screams and wails at nightmares,
Requiring the dispersal of
Monsters and fire breathing dragons,

A bump and clunk from the kitchen,
The ice-box yielding transient
Refueling for teenage growth spurts,

Long awaited creaks on the stairs,
Despite attempted muffling,
After a far past curfew date,

The slam of a car door, hopefully,
Signaling the completion of
A worrisome trip home from college.

In a house suddenly more empty,
Uneasiness comes with the night,
With the silence we hear in the dark.

Reminders

A transparent reflection in a window,
Fading when focused upon, he stands there
At the periphery of my consciousness,
Ever ready to leap out and grab me
With a jolt or a with a gentle start,
Like the tiny Trick-or-Treater,
Too excited to stand still, from whose
Hobgoblin mask shine dancing, sparkling eyes
Just like his.

Working It Out

In grief it seems my tasks are three:
To rethink my faith so it will last,
To live in today and not the past,
But hardest of these jobs to me:
To make sense out of absurdity.

past, present, FUTURE

Life must be lived in precarious balance,
Delicately poised between back then and when.
Why did I then, in seeming control, insist on
Speeding the endless appearing highway ahead,

The present just a peripheral blur
Flashing by as I frantically flew
Down the road on the way to somewhere,
Putting distance between me and back there?

Determined instead to get farther along,
Intent on hurdling the horizon
Or getting to that next bend beyond,
Where I'd find whatever it was I sought.

In my driven, habitual hurry
I missed wandering lanes, shaded pull-offs,
Meandering creeks, bald-headed hills and
Grassy meadows to run or lie down on.

Then, when the lights went out, when sudden darkness fell,
I skidded, crazily careening out of control,
Swearing and crying and wondering how
I could contend with the unbearable Now.

Gentle Reminders

With gentle reminders I am blest,
Soft surprises on me are pressed,
As when I, gazing at the moon,
Feel your presence as my guest.

When I hear the cry of a loon,
Or catch a brief snatch of a tune
That we once shared some time ago,
You seem so near, I'm not alone.

I sense your breath as breezes blow
And your soft kiss in flakes of snow.
In mists sometimes your form I see,
Or in the sunset's afterglow

I often feel you here with me.
Your soul from body now set free
Has the welcome ability
Gentle reminders to bring to me.

Notes From Beyond

Don't cry over me, Mom and Dad,
We are only apart for a while.
I think of you without being sad
And hope when you remember me you smile.

Where I am now is hard to explain.
From your side there are just hints from above,
A vague sense of knowing, deep in your brain,
A place or a time you are not sure of.

In my earlier state, while still in the womb,
I vaguely perceived something outside of you.
You know as much of this side of the tomb,
As beyond my fetal home I then knew.

I've been here forever, I only just came.
Eternity turns time around somehow.
Yesterday, tomorrow, today are the same.
Time is not linear, always is now.

Regarding my end, please set your mind free,
That I was young and my time was not due.
The concept of age and of fairness to me
Is as puzzling as "Why" is to you.

I know life seems indifferent and justice seems gone,
Innocents suffer and men live in fear.
Though all seems hopeless, God's work is not done,
It all fits together when seen from here.

Death dismantles your life, ends all your joys,
Pointless and tragic to mortals it seems.
But dissonant chords and mind piercing noise,
God can arrange into harmonious themes.

It seems very odd that I'm teaching you,
As you once taught me before,
But I want you to know before you come through,
Death's not an end but a door!

So, until your time comes to join me here,
Live your life to the fullest each day.
When you cross over, there's nothing to fear,
For I will be waiting to show you the way.

Getting Better

"You're like your old self,"
They all say to me,
"You're almost back
Like you used to be."
Tears don't come as quick
As they used to do.
They all say I'm better,
It must be true.
Still, there are some things
Of which nobody knows,
Like the box in the closet
That's full of his clothes.

Shadow Grief

A momentary dimming,
Perceived, but not consciously seen,
Puzzlement broken by a shrill overhead cry.
"Ah!" A hawk-eclipse,
As it silently soars
Between me and the sun.

In the echoes of grief
Occasions daily occur,
Moments of happiness
Fleetingly diminished, when
For no obvious reason
A shadow of grief flits by.
Events, still fun and enjoyable,
Are subtly shaded,
The edge of exuberance dulled,
Sepia tinted old movies
Lacking that sparkling sheen,
Engaging, but not quite complete.
Life always seems prefaced by
"Yes, but...."

Family Circle

In my family there are many roles
To be filled: some play Provider, Peacemaker,
Problem Solver, Helper and Healer,
Others are Encourager, Comforter, Nurturer,
And still others Fixer, Learner and Teacher.
But given the cast that we depend on,
Who stands in when the Fun-maker's gone?

I Hope I Believe

I hope we are part of an
Eternal plan, if such a thing
There is. I hope that someday
I will understand why, if there is
A why that exists. I hope
I believe what I say that I do.
I hope what I believe is true.

I believe the quality of life
Is not in its length, but in the
Depth and the breadth that it has.
I believe there is something beyond
This life that we can look forward to.
I believe that there will come a time
When I will once more have dreams.
I believe that there is some One or
Some Thing that cares and comforts me.
And I believe the Source of Good things
In the past still is, and yet will be.

Fare Thee Well

"Fare thee well." Godspeed you on your gentle way,
A sunset's golden glow at close of day,
Imperceptibly fading as it departs
Leaving lasting imprints on our hearts.
I'd have done much more had I but known
You were going. One more word of praise,
One more hug, one more long, loving gaze,
One more touch, one more kiss before you'd gone.

"Fare thee well." That you left in your prime
Assures that never will come the time
That long-lived others come to at last
When their honours and fame are in the past.
But mountains of platitudes cannot hide
That you're not here, whatever you'd be,
Hero or scoundrel, no difference to me.
Better that, than accepting you're gone, you died.

"Fare thee well." We remember you yet.
Those whom you touched can never forget.
As with all who have lived, in time you will fade,
But you will live on in the difference you made
With each kindly act, each word of cheer,
With each friendly smile, each helping hand,
Each act of fairness to a downtrodden man.
Through these, though you're gone, you'll always be here.

"Fare thee well." Since you left, life has stood still.
I've mourned and wept and struggled until
My sadness and grief I've almost worked through.
I think I can live as you would want me to.
There's no way I've found to change your leaving,
But now three long years have past and gone.
The time has come. I must move on
With life and ease away from grieving.

"Fare thee well." Even as you soar up out of sight,
Come visit me in the still of night.
Though I've made a truce with the fact of death,
My spirit would rise if I sensed your breath
Speaking softly to me, new secrets to tell
About where you are and where you have been.
Then I'll whisper back, "Till I'm with you again,
Fare thee well, my darling child,
Fare thee well."

Ghost Story

"Daddy, Daddy, come go with me, please."
To others it's only the wind in the trees,
But in the soft haze of dusk when the mind runs free,
The ghost in the woods is calling to me.
He's spoken often since we've been apart,
In a voice heard not with my ears but my heart.
Down familiar, overgrown pathways he leads
Me to the creek where wood ducks nest in the weeds.
"Over here. Over Here." By the ghost I'm drawn
Into the thicket where he once found a fawn,
White spots on brown in a thick bed of leaves,
Had he not shown me I would have believed
It was bare. "Look up, Daddy, look. It's still there."
The frayed end of the rope swing high in the air
Dangles, unused since he left. Just beyond,
Past the spring and the meadow lies the pond.
"Come. Come." Running ahead, he leads me there
To the sunken log in the corner where
He caught his first fish. I stand, now alone,
While darkness deepens, then slowly head home,
Hearing his voice fade into the haunting call
Of the owl. I stroll through the dark and with hope recall
How a few past times before my walk was done,
I experienced something beyond belief,
As, wholly engulfed by memories and love, for a brief
Magic moment, I and the ghost became one.

Tapestry

Perhaps life is but a tapestry
Far larger than the sky,
Stretching in panoramic splendor from
The dawn of time until suns die.

Perhaps each of us is a single thread,
Into the tapestry briefly woven and
Blended with related fibers forming
A splotch of harmonized beauty,
Lending transient continuity.

Perhaps, beyond our comprehension,
A thread may seem to end before it should,
Disrupting the entire tapestry
With a chaotic clot of clashing color,
A snarled, frayed, broken end,
Leaving doubt there is a guiding hand,
Or, if so, it fumbles and has lost its skill.

Perhaps no single thread is ever lost
But just emerges on the other side
Where the Weaver, with patient, loving hands
Resumes the ageless masterpiece
In a blessed new beginning.

Perhaps we, in eternity,
Will be given the eyes to see
Scenes we were born imagining.

Hidden Treasure

I gather up my memories,
They are all of him that I have.
In my heart there is a treasure chest
Where each one I hoard and save.

At times I have a desperate need
To get away, to sit alone,
And rummage through my memories
Of his life and what is gone.
Then I open up my treasure chest
And with love and tender care,
One by one I take them out,
Dust them off, and replace them there.

Sometimes I go treasure hunting
Through mental backwaters, where
I'm sure I had a memory
That I carelessly left back there.
Rarely, with diligent digging,
It turns up and is mine to hold,
But usually it stays buried,
As lost as the Dutchman's gold.

I am convinced that all around me
There are memories that remain.
Numerous tiny incidents,
Many little events mundane
Lie still to be discovered,
Often triggered in my brain
By a word, a tune or a picture
Which all at once brings them back again.

In the corner of some dark closet,
In a drawer, or under a bed,
Many precious memories lie
Overlooked, perhaps, but not dead.
For a small forgotten memory,
Like a nut hid by a squirrel,
May pop up and surprise me,
And for a moment light my world.

So I will live my life expectantly,
Since, given the vagaries of the mind,
I am sure there are still many
Treasures left, that I have yet to find.

Would You?

To love is to risk,
With risk may come loss,
And loss is full of pain.
In full knowledge of this,
Would I want to go back
And do it all over again?

That we ever had you
Was a gift undeserved,
Unexpected and unearned,
An answer to prayers,
A completeness and wholeness
For which we had yearned.

The time that we shared
Was the Spring of my life,
But I expected Summer and Fall.
Still, if forced to choose,
I'd take Springtime alone,
Than to never have known you at all.

Memorial

"He lives on in those his life touched."
Bronze words set upon a stone
Sound so simple but imply much
More. Whatever you would have done
Will never be. Yet, perhaps
You are kinsman of him who gave
Johnny his first pouch of apple seeds
And caused a continent to blossom.
I, too, plant seeds. From the love we
Gave and received, from the memories
Of the life we shared, have come
Seeds of kindness, tolerance and peace,
Given by you to me. I will plant
And gently tend them in the hard,
Rocky places, the dry places.
And as I do, each seed I plant
Will be in remembrance of you.

Publisher's Note:

The author's world was turned upside down in June 1992 when his youngest son, Bradley, a star college athlete and honor student, was randomly chased down and brutally murdered by young hoodlums. To help overcome his grief, the author became active in The National Conference of Compassionate Friends (a self-help group of parents who have lost children) and wrote poetry as a form of self-therapy. *Rachel's Cry* evolved from his working through the stages of grief—shock, denial, confusion, anger, guilt, depression, turning point and restoration. The result is highly acclaimed and comforting to those whose lives are in the midst of grief. Typical reader responses include:

♦ **This book documents a wrenching journey and is a gift to others. The honesty and imagery offer a moving view into the heart and soul of parents' grief over the loss of a child.**

> D.S. - Oak Ridge, TN

♦ ***Rachel's Cry* is so powerful that I digest it emotionally in small amounts and will reread it many times.**

> I. F. - Eugene, OR

♦ **I read your book and will treasure it always.**

> M. L. - Knoxville, TN

♦ **You say so well what hundreds of us feel but are unable to write. Thanks for sharing your gift.**

> C.P. - Brandon, MS

Rachel's Cry Order Form

I would like to order _____ copies of *Rachel's Cry*. The purchase price is $12.00 per copy. This pays for the book, postage and handling. *Tennessee residents must add 83¢ per copy for state sales tax.*

Send check or money order to:
Tennessee Valley Publishing, P.O. Box 52527, Knoxville, Tennessee 37950-2527.

Discounted prices are available for the purchase of ten or more books. For details call
Tennessee Valley Publishing at 423-584-5235 or E-mail: tvp1@ix.netcom.com

Name _____

Street _____

City _____

State _____ Zip Code _____

Please send book(s) to the following address(s):

Name _____

Street _____

City _____

State _____ Zip Code _____